BUCK'S TOOTH

Diane Kredensor

SCHOLASTIC INC.

ISBN 978-0-545-94388-8

12 11 10 9 8 7 6 5 4 3 2 1   16 17 18 19 20 21

Printed in the U.S.A.   40

First Scholastic printing, January 2016

Designed by Karina Granda
The illustrations for this book were rendered digitally.
The text of this book was set in Avenir LT Std and Grandma.

For Dana and Tina—my Pearls

—D. K.

CHAPTER ONE

This is Buck. He's a beaver.

Like most beavers, Buck had little ears,
a flat tail, thick brown fur, and
big front teeth.

Or in Buck's case, one big,
square front tooth.

Buck didn't like his tooth.

Not one bit.

That tooth ruined everything!

How Buck talked.

How Buck smiled.

How Buck ate.

It did make brushing his teeth easier,
but that was about it.

And now, Buck's big, square tooth was about to
ruin the BIGGEST event of the year—

The Beaverton Talent Show.

No one in Beaverton would think of missing it.

Once, Jimmy Nagel blew such a big bubble, he flew up into a tree.

Everyone is still talking about when Charlie Lane wiggled his ears, tail, and nose while juggling four apples.

This year Buck and his friends were finally
old enough to enter the show.

I'm singing
"Feathers in the Nest."

I'm making my cousins
Ethan and Eddie disappear.

I'm log rolling.

Donald turned to Buck.

What are you going to do, Buck?

Buck looked from Donald
to Pearl to Marvin.
"It's a surprise," he said.

CHAPTER TWO

And it was a surprise.
Even to Buck.
He had no idea what his talent was.

Everything he tried to do ended in disaster.

Stilt walking.

Flute playing.

Whistling.

His tooth always got in the way.
Why did Buck have this silly tooth in the first place?

When Buck's tooth had started to grow, it looked different from everyone else's teeth in his family.

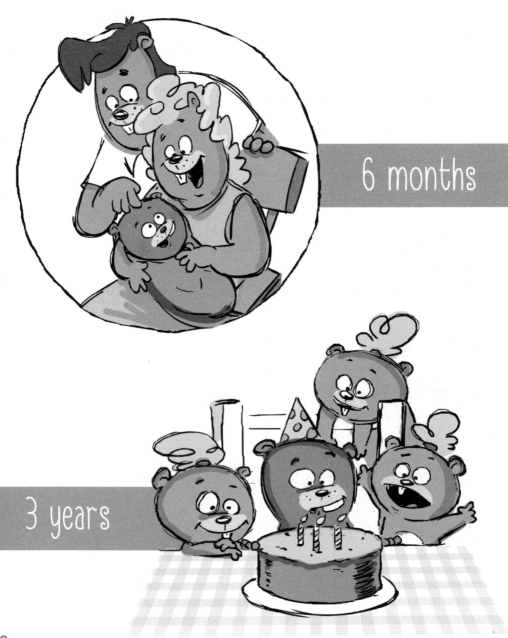

6 months

3 years

Everyone but . . .

His uncle Henry.

Buck looked exactly like him.

Uncle Henry was a famous sculptor. With his one big tooth he could sculpt just about anyone in Beaverton.

Sammy Squirrel
"AMAZING!"

BEAVERTON NEWS
Henry does it again!

Henry scuplts squirrel.

By CHARLIE KILL

Charlie Chipmunk
"INCREDIBLE!"

Henry win
first prize

Tweets B. Bird
"SUPER!"

1st

Bobby Bear
"YOWZA!"

Everyone thought Buck should
follow in Uncle Henry's footsteps.

This is your very first talent show, Bucky.

I remember my first show— I made a toothpick.

What will you be doing?

statue for Talent Show
25th Anniversary

15 FT

BEAVERTON

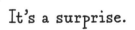

It's a surprise.

Buck stopped.

For the first time in days, he smiled.

That's it!
I have to PULL my tooth OUT!

Buck was sure if he got rid of his tooth,
he would find his talent.

CHAPTER THREE

Buck hurried home and started planning
Operation Tooth Pull.

The next morning, he and his tooth were ready.

Buck started with Plan A. He called his sisters.

Plan A didn't work.

Buck moved on to Plan B.

After opening . . .

thirty pecans,

twenty-two Brazil nuts,

and fifteen walnuts,

Buck's tooth still wouldn't budge.
No problem. There was always Plan C.

Buck went to Marvin's house.

Marvin, I need your help. You're such an awesome magician.

Can you make my tooth disappear?

28

Are you sure, Buck?
I really like your tooth.

Once it's gone, it's
not coming back.

Buck was sure.

He closed his eyes. He took a deep breath
and bid farewell to his tooth.

Hocus pocus!

Buck opened his eyes.
His tooth was still there.

Try again.

Sim sala bim!

Buck's tooth was still there.

No matter what Marvin said, *nothing* happened.

Operation Tooth Pull was officially a failure.

CHAPTER FOUR

Buck wanted to be alone. He went to
one of his favorite spots and crawled in.

Buck started to fall asleep when
he heard Pearl calling his name.

Buck didn't answer.

Finally, Buck spoke.

The surprise is that
I have no talent.

All I have is a big tooth, and both
of us are good at nothing.

That's not true, Buck.

Oh, really?

Have you seen me
play the flute?
Or walk on stilts?
Or eat corn?

At first, Pearl was silent.
But before she left, she told Buck,

You just haven't found your talent yet.

It might be that it's right under your nose.

Once he was alone again, Buck couldn't stop thinking.

Everyone is going to grow up
and leave me behind.

Pearl will be a famous singer.

CHAPTER FIVE

While everyone waited for the talent show to begin . . .

Uncle Henry wheeled
his statue to the back of the stage.

Back at the log, Buck could hear
clapping, laughing, and cheering.
And then he heard singing. It was Pearl!

CHAPTER SIX

Frankie McSunders had just finished reciting "Casey at the Bat."

Fine job, Frankie.

And now Henry Broadtail invites you all to see his newest masterpiece.

The crowd gasped.

Uncle Henry smiled.

I've never seen such fine carving.

The details are amazing.

Bucky, how did you do this?

All eyes were on Buck.

Buck realized what he had said.
Then Buck realized what he had done.

And just like Pearl had said,

Buck's talent was right under his nose the whole time.